Alpha OWNED

This book is a work of fiction. The names, characters, places, and incidents are fictitious or have been used fictitiously, and are not to be construed as real in any way. Any resemblance to persons, living or dead, actual events, locales, or organizations is entirely coincidental.

Published By
Latin Goddess Press
New York, NY 10456
http://millytaiden.com
ALPHA OWNED

Cover by Willsin Rowe

ISBN: 150757178X
ISBN 13: 9781507571781

BBW PARANORMAL ROMANCE

New York Times & USA Today Bestselling Author

MILLY TAIDEN

One

"I really don't like my family or weddings… or men right now." A groan rushed up her throat. Ciara almost choked on her drink trying to tamp down the flare of anger she felt.

"Ciara Ortiz! Calm down. You'd think something horrible was happening the way you're being so dramatic. Honey, it is not the end of the world. It's just a wedding."

Most of the time it was easy to pay attention to Sara's soothing voice. Not this time. All she wanted to do- that her mom would probably not allow- is smack the shit out of her brother at the wedding. His wedding, a wedding his best friend would attend. Ryker Snow.

Alpha to the Snow Mountain Pack, which happened to be the same pack her family belonged to. But did he have to be a sexy bastard too? Yep. Such an injustice. To make matters worse, he also happened to be the man she wanted since grade school. Oh, but it got better. She'd had a never-ending crush on him since their one date fifteen years ago. The damn wedding was giving her nightmares and she wasn't even in the bridal party.

"I'm sure that your family won't really go all fierce and furry if you don't bring a date." Sara patted her hand with a smile. She had that 'I am so damn happy I'm not part of your family' look. And why wouldn't she be? She didn't have to deal with this, Ciara did.

"I'm pissed I have to be part of these archaic traditions."

Sara took a sip of her cocktail and stared at Ciara with her bright hazel eyes. "Bringing a date to a wedding isn't archaic."

Sometimes she wondered if Sara forgot she was human. "If I don't bring a date, they'll start sending single males of the growly type to my house. Possibly even Ryker himself. My mother has always liked him way too much for me."

"My family never sends me single males." Sara grinned.

"That's because you lie to them over the phone about having dates and they don't know any better so they believe you. Your parents will catch on one day and when they do..."

Sara's face paled. "I'm not a shifter. I'm a hybrid of human and shifter and I can't shift!"

Ciara sucked down some more of her martini. "Doesn't matter. Your parents are going to be sending you a bunch of tall sexy, 'I am wolf hear me roar' single males when they realize you've been playing them."

"They won't." She tried to sound sure, but Ciara heard the wobble in her voice.

Jeez. What the fuck was wrong with her? Next she'd start kicking puppies and shit. Poor Sara. She wanted a mate as much as Ciara wanted to see Ryker.

"I still think it's kind of cool that your mom mated a shifter like my mom. Your step-dad is the right hand to the new Alpha smokin' sexy guy we all know. Bad boy with hot body also known as Ryker Snow."

Ciara chugged down the cosmopolitan the waitress had put before her a second ago and raised her hand for her to bring another. Shit just got real. Sara didn't live with the pack, but she visited a lot more often than Cici did. Sara loved bringing back details on what the family was up to since Ciara took forever to go back.

Ryker. The Alpha. Christ, she needed to stop thinking of him or she'd end up drunk, laying by a toilet and crying into the bathroom mat. She'd had one date with the man that went south the moment word got out at school. They hadn't even had their date and she'd been warned off Ryker. One of the girls had told Ciara he'd never see her as a mate. Sexy man Ryker needed a shifter to lead the pack. Lovely. What was the point of seeing him after that?

"Good point. So then just bring someone. Heck, hire a man and take him as your date. They already know you live among the humans and have little to do with the shifter world."

Ciara's phone beeped at the same moment their good friend Darius joined them. A text message popped up on her screen from her mother.

I hope you come to your brother's wedding this weekend. You know we miss you and can't wait to see you.

Darn it. There went telling her mom she was sick. It wasn't her mom's fault she was human. Her mom had been human too, until she mated Ryan, her step-dad, and turned. Being the only one in the family unable to shift sucked. She was used to it, though. Her mom married Ryan back when she was a little girl so she'd grown up around shifters. She'd been more fascinated with them than they had been with her. Actually, the females had really disliked her when she was growing up.

"Hey, chicas." Darius kissed them on both cheeks. It was his favorite way to greet friends.

"Oh!" Sara's eyes went so wide Ciara thought they'd pop out of her head.

"What?" Darius and Ciara asked at the same time.

"Take Darius!" She wiggled on her seat, long dark curls bouncing with her.

"Take me where?" Darius' dark head whirled back and forth between the two of them like someone following a game at a ping-pong match.

"What?" Ciara exclaimed, a lot louder than necessary. Things got confusing there. She'd only had a few…or six drinks and not enough to lose track so quickly.

"It's the perfect plan." Sara leaned forward on the table, glancing between Darius and Ciara.

"What plan? Take her where?" Poor Darius sounded so lost. Almost as lost as Ciara felt with Sara's crazy plan.

"She needs a date for her brother's wedding. So you should take her."

"Why not take a real date?"

Ciara rolled her eyes. "Because I don't have one. I haven't had a real date in months. Have you forgotten I work crazy hours?"

Face creased in sympathy, he nodded. "You do work crazy hours, but you're a baker, so it's understandable."

"Thank you. So you see why I have no man?"

"Which is why you should take him." Sara chimed in again.

"What's the big deal? Aren't you going to this wedding, Sara? As far as I know you don't have a man either."

Sara reeled back and folded her arms over her chest. "I don't have a man, but my parents think I do. He is traveling overseas and won't be able to attend the wedding."

"Perfect timing." Ciara muttered.

There went her sarcasm again. She needed to get slapped. Maybe she could use that as an excuse to skip the dreaded wedding.

"Seriously, guys," Sara glanced back and forth between them, "you need a date." She pointed her cocktail at Ciara. "And you owe her from the time she got you those last minute cupcakes."

"Great time to bring it up." Darius groaned.

"That's true. You do owe me. Those cupcakes were the sole reason your parents didn't freak out when you told them they should stop trying to hook you up with women if they ever wanted you in a relationship. Remember?"

"Yeah, yeah. I told them if they wanted to hook me up to focus on some of the hot guys at my dad's firm." He smiled at the waitress and took his own cocktail out of her hands. "Those cupcakes stopped what was clearly an uncomfortable moment to a more relaxed chat."

Happiness filled Ciara's chest. She loved that something small she'd made had helped Darius come out of the closet. He'd let his super religious family know he was a happily gay man and he wasn't going to change.

"You don't have to do it, D." Defeat pulled at Ciara's muscles. Her first time seeing Ryker in almost fifteen years wouldn't be pretty. She pressed the bridge of her nose and shut her eyes. Shit. The last thing she wanted was to look like some loser who didn't have a man. Not to mention what her mom or step dad would resort to once they realized she was single. They'd probably slip a guy into every second of the weekend. "I think I need another drink."

Darius laughed. His golden brown skin very similar to her own Latin one glowed. "Ciara Ortiz! I got your back girl. I'll pretend to be your boyfriend, fiancé, whatever you need. Heck I'll be your husband or a baby daddy if you want."

Sara choked on her laughter. "Baby daddy? Her parents would know if she was pregnant. They'd scent it. I think you guys should just do the whole engaged best friends deal. I bet that will work best."

Darius kissed the top of Ciara's head. "I already love you to death, so this won't be too hard."

A smile split Ciara's lips. She glanced up into his dark chocolate eyes. "You love me like a sister, not some chick you want to have your babies."

"Hey, I took drama in college. I can channel my inner heterosexual."

"This is going to be so interesting." Sara laughed, still bouncing in her seat.

Two

Ryker stared at his beer in thought. "Do you think she'll come?"

Christian, his best friend and right hand man gulped down his own beer. "You never know with Cici. One day she says yes and the next she says no. She's probably trying to figure out how to get out of it."

Ryker grinned. "She can't. It's your wedding. She has to come."

He was counting on her showing up. That had been his biggest wish since she'd moved away. For her to return just once so he could make her his. But Ciara wasn't some timid little woman. She had bigger balls than most men he knew. She also had something against being near or alone with Ryker. Ryker had yet to figure out what caused her frostiness toward him. They'd had a single date which, even he had to admit, had been the worst ever, but he knew she was the one for him.

"You sound just like my mother. She's bought Ciara's favorite wine. Ten bottles of it. I don't know what she expects her to do with all that wine. I mean, she's only here for a few days."

No. Not a few days, if Ryker had his way. Ciara would be staying because she belonged with him. That was the reality of things. As Alpha of the Snow Mountain Pack, Ryker had been offered every female, but he'd refused them all. Ciara was who he wanted. The only one.

"Is there anything about her life in the city I should know about?" He asked.

Christian popped a pretzel into his mouth and winced. "She says she has a boyfriend."

What? "Is it true?"

Christian shrugged. "You never know with Ciara. She could be making it up just so we don't badger her about finding a man. Mom always tends to take every conversation in that direction. Your name usually falls in the line of possible candidates."

Ciara with a boyfriend? That wasn't good. Ciara was his. The wolf inside him pushed at his skin wanting loose. He wanted to hunt down the man Ciara said was her boyfriend and get rid of the competition. She was his. There was not going to be any more fighting it from her side.

Ryker had given her time but she was sneaky. She'd made sure to only visit when he wasn't at the mountain. She'd gone as far as to do visits when her brother was gone. He wasn't sure, but Ryker had a feeling it was because she knew that meant Ryker wouldn't be there either.

Christian didn't let Ryker travel alone. He always had his back. Especially when he went to visit other packs. Even though most were friendly with the Snow Pack, Christian didn't like to take chances. Ryker stopped debating with his friend that he could take care of himself. Christian was his right hand man and he did the job damn well.

He could have chased Cici. Gone to find her and brought her back to his home as his woman. But Ryker thought Ciara would prefer to be given the chance to come to terms with her future. She'd be his mate. There was no denying that. He'd said that to her on their one date and it had ended with her telling him she wasn't a shifter and he needed to find another girl. She'd been a teen so he thought time would change her outlook. It seemed time was the last thing she'd needed.

He planned to spend time with Ciara during this visit. She needed to see that things between them, was the right path for her to take. That being his mate was nothing for her to be afraid of but the right choice for her.

"Is Michelle ready to finally tie the knot?" Ryker asked moving the conversation to Christian and his bride to be.

Christian grinned. "She's excited. I think she's more excited that she won't have her ex in her life anymore."

The abusive ex. Poor Michelle. Christian's fiancée had been in such a bad short-lived relationship she'd tried to change her identity in order to move on and keep the devil away. Thankfully, Christian being a shifter, was more than able to protect Michelle. She hadn't taken to the change. So she needed Christian to help protect her from the evil ex and any other man who tried to put his hands on her.

"Michelle is a good woman. I'm glad you found her."

Christian lifted his beer bottle and took a long drink. "Mom keeps talking about you and Ciara. She wants you to finally take her for a mate. Says you've waited too long and now Cici might not want to return here for the long term."

That was a possibility. But he knew Ciara deep down. She was a family person. All the time she'd lived in the pack had shown him that she didn't like being away from her mother and brother. She'd done it to prove her independence and to stay away from Ryker. There was no need for her to stay away any longer.

Ryker would show her how welcomed she was in his pack. In his life. And in his bed. She was his mate. He'd known it since they were kids on a bad date.

Ciara gnawed at her lip as they left her house. The three decided to drive their way back to Snow Mountain. Not fond of small planes, Sara begged and the others relented. It wasn't much begging either, since Ciara was more than happy to lengthen the hours before she saw the pack.

"What did you two decide on then? Married, divorced," Sara glanced at Cici from the driver's seat, wiggling her brows provocatively. "Living in sin and enjoying every minute?"

Darius and Cici laughed. They couldn't help it. Thinking of both of them saying they were having hot sex to anyone was as ridiculous as saying Ciara was going on a new diet. Cici didn't do diets. She was a big girl with big curves and loved each and every one of them. Darius didn't do chicks. It was like that.

"You know what, Ciara?"

She turned in her seat to glance at him in the back seat. He lay with his plush foam pillow under his arm.

"What's up, baby doll?"

"If I ever think of being with a woman, you'd be my first choice."

Aw. Darius was so sweet. Sara and Cici knew he'd had a hard time telling his family he was gay, which was why they loved helping him open up and be whoever he wanted to be. "I know honey. But if at any point you feel uncomfortable with things, just tell me and we'll pull the plug, okay?"

He frowned. "I'd never back out on you. You're my best friend."

That's why Cici loved Darius. He and Sara had forever been her unconditional friends. More than she could have hoped for. They didn't care that she was a big girl that came from a strange family of shifters. Granted, Sara had her own shifter family in which she was the only one that didn't shift. But Cici had a mother who wanted grandchildren. And in the shifter community, curves were much appreciated. So her mother tried repeatedly to mention every eligible shifter male in the pack, but never mentioned Ryker. He was the only one Cici wanted. Throat bone dry, she turned back to stare at the road.

Things weren't as simple as showing up with Darius. They'd both have to play a game that wouldn't get them caught in lies or they'd smell them. So everyone decided to stick to what they knew. They did love each other, as friends, but nobody needed to know that part.

The surroundings went from big city buildings to small towns and finally to cabins in the woods. That's how the Snow Mountain Pack lived in private cabins, really pretty ones too. The architecture of the cabins was like something out of Ultimate Cabins Magazine. Nobody in the pack wanted for money, so homes were large, comfortable and breathtaking. The whole set up was surreal. Thick large trees surrounded the cabins with oranges and browns on each of the fall leaves blending perfectly to create a canvas of warm colors.

"Hot damn!" Darius yelled. "You guys have been holding out on me. Are you girls billionaires or something?"

Sara giggled. "No. We're not, but our parents have some money."

Sara drove her 4x4 through the high ground, until they reached the highest level on the mountain. Several cabins sat in a semi-circle in the large clearing.

"Jesus. So who lives in these?" Awe filled Darius' voice.

Cici smiled at Sara and let her gaze roam over the beauty before them. Cici decided to answer Darius as simply as possible. Shifter leadership still confused her. "To the left is my parents' cabin. My father used to be the old Alpha's, Ryker's dad's, top enforcer, but moved to the role of advisor and elder for Ryker. That gives him some kind of seniority. Now my brother Christian is Ryker's top enforcer." With a quick glance over her shoulder, Cici grinned at the stupefied look on Darius' face. "What I mean is that Christian is in charge of all the guards. Those two smaller cabins behind my parent's house are for guests like me. Yes, I consider myself a guest." Though she made it a point to only visit when she knew Ryker wasn't around. "That middle cabin, the big one, that's Ryker's."

"The guy you've had the hots for since grade school?"

Sara burst into laughter, slapping her hands on the wheel. "Yeah. That one."

"Cut it out. It wasn't since grade school. I'm your future baby mama, remember?" Cici joked.

"True. Sorry to have interrupted, my love. Please go on."

Ryker's cabin was gorgeous. Two stories of absolute beauty made with wood and glass. And every time she visited she could only wish to own something that amazing one day.

"That cabin to the right of Ryker's belongs to Sara's parents. Her dad was Ryker's dad's beta, but he's retired and is also advising Ryker as his elder. Sara's brother, Sean, took on the duty for Ryker."

"And they also keep little cabins for you, Sara darlin', I see." Darius pointed out.

Sara giggled. "Yeah. They know I stay up late and wake up late. These people sleep so little it's annoying."

"Not to mention the loud animal sex." Cici snorted.

"Ciara!" Sara's hand slapped her shoulder, leaving a stinging spot on her skin.

"Come on. You know it's true. Our families are loud when they have sex and it's why our parents allowed us to keep our cabins separate when we were old enough to tell them we didn't want to hear them anymore."

Darius laughter filled the vehicle. It was infectious and had Cici laughing in seconds. The sounds calmed down some of the nerves that were turning her muscles to stone.

"Okay, you're right. I hated having to hear that shit."

A quick peek over her shoulder and she saw Darius wiping at his cheeks. He'd laughed that hard. "So let me see if I got this straight. Left side is Cici's family of enforcers and elder. Right side is

Sara's family of Betas and elder. And middle is sexy pants Ryker growly Alpha?"

"You got it in one!" Cici chuckled. "And you weren't even drinking."

"Uh-oh." Sara groaned. "The Calvary has arrived."

Both sets of parents closed in on the 4x4. Cici's beautiful mother, who she swore hadn't aged a single year since she turned, ran for them, a wide smile covered her face.

Homesickness filled Cici then. She'd missed her so much. A knot formed in her throat as she struggled with her shaking hands to open the door. Hopping out faster than she'd ever thought possible, she ran for her mom too. In a blur of movement, Cici was enveloped in the warmth and love only her mother could show. She hugged her tight, so tight it was like she was afraid to let Cici go.

"Ciara, my baby." Her mother whispered, voice thick with tears.

"I missed you, mom." Cici choked out. She needed to stop this insanity. Ryker was going to be Alpha leader of their pack for a long time. It was time to let that shit go and visit her family more often.

Hot tears slid down her cheeks. She saw herself in her mother's golden eyes and knew that she suffered because she missed Cici.

"I missed you too, baby girl."

"I won't do this anymore." The promise shot from Cici's lips without a trace of hesitation. "I'll come see you more often."

Her smile lit her eyes until they glowed. "I hope so."

"There's other people here. Can we get in on the hugging too?" Her brother cut in.

Her mom let go of her. Then her super tall and muscular baby brother hugged her half to death.

"Christian! I can't breathe." She wheezed as he turned her around in fast dizzying circles.

Her mother and brother all of a sudden stopped and turned to meet her third friend with a frown.

"Hi, I'm Darius." He introduced himself to Cici's mother.

"Welcome to our land. Are you and Ciara close?" Her mom asked. Eyeing Darius with intense scrutiny.

"More than close. There are no words to tell you what she means to me."

"Oh, wow." Her mom's voice came out a surprised squeak. Yeah. Ciara knew her mother had always wanted Ciara to hook up with Ryker so this was going to put a damper on her plans.

Chris put Cici back on her feet with care. "I missed you, Ciara. Stay here with us. Forget going back to that smog-infested city. You can bake to your heart's delight here. We do like sweets you know."

"I know. It's why I'm early. Michelle asked me to bake your groomsman cake remember?"

A deep frown marred his brow and Cici saw the animal bright in his eyes. "I don't want you to work. I want you to relax."

"Cut it out, Chris! I love baking. That's how I relax."

At that moment, Chris stared deep into her eyes. A chill ran down her spine. "You're coming home to stay, soon."

The way he said the words, with so much assurance, freaked her out a little. She would visit more, that was already decided, but he said come home to stay. That was a lot more complicated. Something tightened in her chest. Pain gnawed at her gut. She'd neglected her family long enough.

"I'm sorry, Chris. We'll make your wedding special, little brother. That was the mission. To ensure the family had a great time at Chris and Michelle's wedding.

Sara's mom went on and on about the need to finally meet Sara's boyfriend. Cici felt horrible for Sara. She knew if she said anything they'd know she'd been lying. Cici decided to help her. Holding on to Chris's hand, she took a few steps toward Sara and her mom Rosa.

"Hi, Rosa. I see you look as fantastic as you did the last time we saw you."

Rosa smiled at Cici, her dimples showed on her smooth wrinkle-free face. She had warm hazel eyes that always made Cici think of being cuddled in a down comforter.

"Hey, Sara? Want to help us out getting things set up for all the baking I'm doing in the morning?"

"Yes!" She tugged out of Rosa's hold and bounced over to Cici.

"Mom, Darius is staying in the cabin with me."

Her mom's brown skin paled until she appeared a sickly gray. "Are you sure?"

"Yeah. We'll stay together. We have to, you know." She laughed and winked at her, hoping her actions implied what she couldn't say for fear of being found out to be a liar.

"Sure sure." She glanced at Chris with wide eyes. "Help set them both up in the other cabin. Let her know what rooms they're in."

"You got it, mama."

Hours later, things had finally settled. They'd had dinner with Cici's family and so far, she'd done a good job of avoiding Ryker. Not that it made a difference since he wasn't in town anyway.

After a nice long bath, her mind and body agreed to let her rest. She opted for some of the wine her mother had left. Once she got going, it was kind of hard to stop.

Every time she thought of facing Ryker, she downed another glass. Pretty soon she had multiple empty bottles littering the kitchen island. Darius had gone to a late night bon fire with Sara. They'd tried to get Cici to join, but after setting up for the following morning's baking, she knew she wasn't going anywhere.

She laid down with her third or fourth bottle of wine, thinking of Ryker and playing out what she'd say to him. Would he tell her he missed her? Probably not. He was too busy being in charge. Soon, he'd be looking for a mate and he probably gave her no thought.

Life sucked. She didn't want to think of Ryker but dammit why did his gorgeous eyes and hot body come to mind? Stupid hormones. Soon, she was drifting off into a wine-induced sleep.

Her visions of Ryker led her to an amazing dream. It had to be a dream because she knew he wasn't in town. Yet there he was. In her bedroom. Looking as good as he had the first time her teenage eyes had fallen for him. This dream had to be brought on by the wine and the incessant thoughts of seeing him again.

"Ciara." Ryker's deep voice sunk into her pores and lit an instant fire in her blood.

Three

"Ryker." His name sounded so right, so perfect dropping from Cici's lips. She'd been dying to say it but had curved the need, until now. She was in her dream world and could do and say anything she wanted.

"That's right, little one. You came back for me." His lips trailed down her jaw, dropping butterfly kisses over her skin. Arousal coiled in her core. Her lungs froze at the feel of his hands sliding under her tank top.

"What are you doing here?" She asked, her muddled mind telling her to forget about questions and to let him do anything he wanted. This was a dream and questions would make it too real.

"I came for you."

This was definitely a dream. No way he'd say that in real life.

"You did? Wow. I love where this is going," she breathed.

He cocked his head and glanced at her lips. "I thought you had a boyfriend. Darius?"

She giggled. Geez. Even in her dreams she had dragged poor D into her lie. "He's just a friend. A good friend, but only a friend. He's my bestest friend. But he's gay. I'm like a sister to him."

"So why are you saying he's your boyfriend?"

Boy, this version of Ryker liked to talk. She wanted to get her sexy fantasy going already. "Who cares, why? Come here and show me you want me."

The room spun on its axis. A hazy vision of him lay on top of her, pressing her body down into the mattress. His gorgeous blue eyes stared deep into hers, so deep she worried he knew her feelings for him. But this was a dream, so it was fine if he found out.

His lips trailed up to meet hers. Passion exploded, dragging her further into the delicious dream.

How often had she had dreams like this? Almost every night. But none of the other times had it felt so real. His touch felt so intense that her dream seemed real, like it was actually happening. She wasn't sure if it was because of all the wine or because she was back home, but this dream was by far the best she'd ever had.

He drew circles on her side with his calloused fingers. The feel of his rough fingers cupping the sides of her breasts made her breath hitch. It didn't stop there, no. That's where it all went crazy. His tongue drove deep into her mouth, rubbing up against hers.

Savage.

Rough.

Delicious.

Almost as if he'd been dying to taste her.

Every caress was like a new dose of pleasure swarming her body. Her nipples tightened. God, the feel of his hands on her breasts shot her temperature through the roof. She moaned into the kiss, lifting her hands up to slide them up his muscular arms. Even in a dream his shifting muscles felt like steel under her palms. The bar of his cock pressed between her legs. She wiggled under his hot body. It felt amazing. And she wanted more. Faster. Now. This was her dream and she wanted him to finally do all the things she'd been fantasizing about.

He tore his lips away from hers. She panted, struggling to catch a single breath.

"Ciara, love."

The fogginess in her brain wouldn't dissipate. The room spun again and she knew then that she'd had way too much wine. A lot more than normal if even in her dream things were unstable. She fought the gravity and dizziness. Instead she helped him take her top off and watched him with awe.

He licked a slow trail down her collarbone to her chest. Breaths struggled into her lungs. His hot lips sucked on her nipple.

"Oh my..." She gasped. "God!"

Loud heartbeats hammered in her chest. Goosebumps broke out all over her skin at the tiny bites and hard sucks. What a dream. If this was something new she never wanted to wake up. Ever. Shit, they might find her asleep for three days so she could make it last.

"You taste fucking delicious, Cici," he growled. "All these curves have been driving me crazy for years. I want to fuck you until I am the only thing I smell on you."

Dear lord, yes!

"Oh, Ryker..."

"That's it," he groaned, biting and sucking her flesh. "I want my cock deep in you. Feeling your pussy wrap around me tight." He bit her again. "I've waited so long for you. Too long. You're mine."

His large hands squeezed her sensitive flesh at the same time he rocked his cock between her legs. Arousal dampened her shorts to the point of being soaking wet. She licked her lips, moaning once again at his amazing skill sucking her nipples. Each suck felt like an electric tug on her clit. Her pussy throbbed, wanting to be filled.

"Please…oh yes…"

"You like this, sweetheart?"

"I love every single touch." She replied honestly. What did it matter anyway? This was a dream. And because it was her dream she felt uninhibited. "Lick my pussy, Ryker. I've waited forever for you to finally touch me. To take me."

He growled, a deep vibration that coursed through her body from his mouth on her tit. He sucked on her nipple hard and her pussy grasped at nothing. Oh, she wanted him so bad.

"I've been waiting for you to tell me that." His deep rough voice melted all her brain cells into putty. "Tell me to fuck you, baby. Tell me you want me in you."

"I do. I want your face between my legs, licking me. Fuck me with your tongue."

Her shorts were yanked off her body. She glanced down at the foggy vision of him. Thick muscles shifted under his lightly tanned arms. Those bulging biceps pushed her thighs wide open as he settled between them. Their gazes met. Possession brightened his blue eyes, making them glow with the power of his wolf. Blazing need made her body shudder.

"Mine," she whispered. This might be the only time she could say that. And she knew the word had deep meaning with shifters. Even though it was a dream, he had to know how badly she wanted him.

His nostrils flared. The lines of his face tightened and sideburns appeared out of nowhere. Another growl and she knew he had a hard time holding his wild side back. Not today. This was her dream.

"Man and wolf, I want you both," she said, still caught in his dominant gaze. His fingers bit deep into her thighs. His tight grip told her he fought to hold on to his human side, to keep the beast at bay. Maybe she was a sick person, but that knowledge increased her lust by too many degrees to count. It was her fantasy and by God he was going to give her all of him.

"Ciara..." The word was an unintelligible garble. Nothing had ever made her feel as powerful as knowing that she made Ryker lose control. Even if it only happened in a dream.

"Eat my pussy. Make me come." She licked her lips. He glanced down at her wet folds. His eyes glowed brighter. "Then, make me yours."

His head dropped between her legs. With a single lick from ass to clit, he strung the tension in her core so tight that she readied to snap. Her eyes shut on their own accord. Stars burst behind her lids with each flutter of his lips on her pussy. He swept his tongue up and down in quick flicks. Dammit. She'd never had a man with a tongue that could work that kind of magic. Then he twirled it in slow circles around her clit, driving the fire in her blood to boiling. Her grip on the dream went out the window at that point.

Time and space blurred into a bunch of flashes of light and sound. Whimpers, groans, and moans, all coming from her, echoed around the room. Ryker dipped two fingers into her pussy, fucking her with them, driving in and out harsh and fast. The same way she imagined he'd fuck her with his cock. Her grip on the sheets loosened. Before she knew it she was pinching her own nipples, adding friction and a bite of pain to the increasing pleasure.

"God, yes. Keep going," she moaned. Screw it. She might wake up on a wet spot out of her own wet dream, but she didn't care. This fantasy had just turned so hot there was no stopping. Forget waking up. She wanted to keep it going.

He growled deep into her pussy. Shakes racked her body with the vibration traveling through her.

Tension curled around the pit of her stomach. More. More. Until all she knew was the urge to fling herself from the cliff she knew would bring her the most amazing climax. Her back curled, lifting off the bed. Her moans increased in volume, each one louder than the last. Fuck, she couldn't breathe. All she knew was the need for the tightness to break.

"I need to come," she begged.

Maybe that's all he needed to hear. As soon as the words left her mouth, he clamped his lips around her swollen clit, suctioning tight and flicking his tongue in rapid-fire sweeps.

She screamed. Loud. In that single moment she saw fireworks, went deaf and lost herself in a wave of pleasure she never knew existed. Her body floated in a sea of bliss. He continued to fuck her with his fingers and she felt his teeth graze her inner thigh in a sharp bite. His small nibble pushed her into a quick succession of mini orgasms. Breaths pushed their way into her lungs. Her knees shook. She knew that she would never have a dream this amazing again.

The orgasmic exhaustion pulled her out of her dream and into a land of relaxation. She wanted to tell him to take her and make things between them even better, but she was tired. Sleep pulled at her muscles. Besides, there would be other dreams where Ryker could do even naughtier things to her than just licking her into orgasm. Ryker kissed her temple and held her tight, snuggling her into his hot body from behind.

"I'm not letting you go."

Had this not been a dream, she would have probably freaked out. But since it was, she let herself wish.

"You don't have to. I only want you."

* * *

Ryker stared at Christian with a wide grin.

"You look like the cat that ate the canary," Christian laughed. "Which leads me to think that your visit to Cici last night was a success?"

Ryker's chest constricted thinking of Cici. She'd been wild. A lot more than she'd ever been before. In fact, other than the fact she'd clearly been drinking, he didn't know what possessed her to be so open to him. "It was great. I marked her."

Christian slapped him on the shoulder. "Congrats, man. I'm so happy for you. I know you've been waiting for her to come around a long time. Seems that she couldn't have been that close to that other guy."

She wasn't. Not only that, but Ryker wouldn't ever think to poach on another man's woman. Even if it was the love of his life. He'd gone down to the bon fire and once he'd told Darius how much he cared for Cici, the other man had been truthful and explained she was unsure of how Ryker felt for her so she'd asked him to pretend to be a couple with her.

At first, he'd been disappointed that Ciara had gone to those lengths to avoid Ryker, but once Darius told him it was because she cared about him and thought Ryker didn't care back, he realized the best way to prove to her how he felt was to go see her.

He hadn't thought they'd end up with him marking her. Hell, the last thing he'd wanted was to push her into anything, but she'd offered herself and he wasn't going to say no. Fuck that. He'd said no to his urges far too many damn times.

"So you think she'll stay here? Be with us?" Christian asked, voicing one of the questions at the front of Ryker's mind.

"I am not sure. I don't want to push her too fast. She had reasons for staying away and I don't want her to feel like I'm expecting her to drop everything and come. That's not where I want us to go."

Christian nodded and fixed the receipts they'd been going through for the new building materials needed to add a new community center to the town.

"Women are tough. Sometimes they tell you what they think, but more often than not, they expect you to guess." He snorted. "Like we're fucking magicians or something."

"I'm not sure what I should do with Cici. I want her to want to stay."

Christian sighed. "I get it. If you tell her you want her to stay she might think you're pushing her to, but if you don't she might think you don't care."

Exactly. Frickin' hell. Women were hard. "I need a drink."

"It's like ten in the morning," Christian laughed. "Let's get some coffee."

He could use coffee and a bottle of vodka. Thinking of Ciara was the highlight of his day but the thought of her rejecting him and not staying at Snow Mountain made him all kinds of worried. She was too independent to be told what to do. She wasn't technically a member of his pack so he had no rule over her. And he didn't want to tell her to stay. That was something she had to choose on her own.

"When you guys went on that one date, shit went down the drain." Christian said, mentioning the only time he and Cici had ever done anything social as kids.

He walked beside Christian to the kitchen in his house. "I wanted her. I think something I said may have pushed her away. She seemed fine at first, but then she went cold on me. Refused to talk and eventually she rejected all my invitations to get together."

Christian filled a mug with coffee. "She mentioned someone telling her that you would only want a shifter for a mate. I guess after that she didn't think she'd have a chance with you."

Fucking hell! If that was the case, that would explain why she had left and pushed him away. She didn't want to be hurt. Ciara wanted him. He knew that. He'd seen it in her eyes. He'd heard it from her lips.

"I'll talk to her. Explain that whatever impression she is under is wrong. That I choose who I want for a mate and that she's the only one I want."

Christian dumped sugar and cream into his coffee, stirring it with a small spoon, the metal clinking as it touched the porcelain of the cup. "You're a better man than most. When Cici decides something it's rare that she changes her mind. It's why she doesn't really have a boyfriend. She has refused relationships and I think it's because of you. Nobody measures up."

Ryker leaned back on the counter and folded his arms over his chest. "I love her. But she's got to be the most stubborn woman in the world."

Christian laughed. "You're telling me? I'm her brother."

"I guess I'll just have to get her to admit her feelings."

Christian lifted the mug to his lips. "Good luck, bro."

He knew he'd need it. Cici was worth it, though. She was his life.

* * *

The next morning, Cici woke up more exhausted than when she laid down with a bottle of wine. Luckily, the bottle had been empty or it would have spilled all over her bed. She'd been well and truly drunk to the point she couldn't remember falling asleep or drinking in bed. There was also the terrible dry mouth and slight headache from her hangover she needed to deal with. Temptation urged her to forget baking and sleep some more. That was the first clue she needed to get up or she'd never do anything.

Neither Sara nor Darius showed up for a while, which was normal since they were both late sleepers. Shit, even Cici loved sleeping in, but the groom's cake for Chris wouldn't wait.

Due to the small oven in the cabin, she'd have to bake in two rounds. That part sucked. She loved being able to shove all her cakes into one large oven and cut the time in half. By the time she'd got the first cake to bake, Darius and Sara made their way into the kitchen.

"Morning." Sara groaned, running her fingers through her mussed up hair.

"Need caffeine." Darius muttered, heading straight for the coffee maker.

"You guys look like you got run over by the vicious sleep fairy. Shit. I thought I'd had it bad when I woke up with a headache earlier."

Darius gave her the finger and Sara dropped her head into her folded arms on the dining room table.

"What happened?" Cici asked. Hands wiped clean, she sat down on the table across from Sara.

"Liquor happened." Her words were muffled from having her head down.

"I don't get it." Cici curled her fingers over the mug Darius handed her and placed it in front of Sara. "What's wrong with liquor? I had my fair share."

"Shifters don't get drunk."

"Okay?" Cici still didn't understand.

"They did a ton of drinking last night at the bon fire. We drank right along with them."

Hangovers. Shifters didn't get drunk. But Sara was mostly human and Darius was fully human. They'd have gotten some bad hangovers if they drank as much as the shifters or tried to keep up. That sucked big time.

"You guys need to drink water and relax." Cici patted Sara's curls. "I need to go into town and buy some stuff I forgot for the second cake batch."

Darius cupped his cheek and sighed. "We'll come with you."

"Yeah." Sara lifted her head and sniffed. Then frowned. She sniffed again and studied her.

"I know I smell like cake and sweat right?" Cici grumbled.

"No. You smell…different." She cocked her head as if looking for something. "But my brain isn't working so well due to the headache and exuding liquor I can smell on myself. Ugh. I hate that this is what I'll smell for the next few hours. My own body trying to get rid of alcohol. Nasty."

"I don't know what you're talking about. I don't smell different." Cici stood and stepped away. "I'll take a shower and we can go."

"You're fine. It's probably all the alcohol messing with my head. I've never drank that much.

Whenever I come back I forget I'm the hybrid with the dominant human genes. I can't even drink like the shifters or I end up wasted."

"Yeah. Let's just go. We'll come back and sleep some more after." Darius blinked repeatedly. It was obvious he needed to rest some more.

Surprise hit her when she realized neither her mother nor her brother had shown up to invite her for breakfast. How odd. One of the things they loved was to spend mornings eating tons of pancakes and talking. For her family, it'd become a tradition whenever she came home. Then again, there's a wedding being planned, so things were probably nowhere near normal.

Their drive down to the middle of the mountain where most of the town resided had been quiet. She knew Sara and Darius needed peace from too much conversation.

People she and Sara knew came up to chat. All of them stared at her with wide eyes and slacked jaws. Cici started to feel uncomfortable. What the hell was wrong with them? She hadn't changed that much since the last time she'd been there. She was still a big, curvy girl and her hair was still the same color. Actually, it was longer now. There was no reason for the shocked gasps.

"What's up with these people?" Cici whispered to Sara.

"I don't know. If one more person hugs me I will throw up all over them." Poor Sara rubbed a hand over her stomach. Her skin had taken a greenish color and her shoulders drooped.

"Let's go. I got the stuff I need and these guys are acting too weird." Darius helped carry the bags to the car, frowning at the gawking spectators.

"Have you all never seen a man with two beautiful women?" He shouted at a group of women huddled by the store's entrance.

Cici refused to let the weird reactions of people she hadn't seen in a while bother her. Most of them were the women who had disliked her as kids. They'd told her repeatedly she was the fat human that couldn't shift. Darius rolled his eyes and got in the back seat. At the same time Cici opened the front passenger side door she heard her name.

Michelle, her future sister in law hurried toward them. She smiled. Though they had met only once before, Cici found her to be really sweet. Plus, she was mostly human. She hadn't taken the change when Christian mated her.

Michelle hugged her tight. She smiled at her enthusiastic welcome.

"Oh!" She reeled back, staring at her with shocked brown eyes.

"What?"

She grinned. "Congratulations!"

What?

"She must have heard we're engaged." Darius winked at her from inside the car.

Oh.

Michelle frowned. "No..." Her eyes went wide. "You're marked."

Four

"Excuse me?"

"That's it!" Sara hollered, rushing to her side of the car, almost running into poor Michelle. "I knew I smelled something different about you but I couldn't put my finger on what. My sense of smell is only a little bit better than that of a human, but not as good as a shifter."

"You are drunk." I pointed out.

"Yeah, but she's not." Sara turned to study Michelle's features. "Are you?"

Michelle chuckled. She shook her head, swinging her long brown hair from side to side. "Not even a little bit."

"So I'm right!" Sara stopped and turned to Cici, her green complexion turned ashy. "Oh my God. How the hell are you marked?"

Unease raced through Cici, settling at the pit of her stomach. She gulped. Her dream. That was the only explanation. She'd never had such a vivid dream about Ryker. But then why was everything so fuzzy? The wine! She'd been drunk as a skunk and thought she was dreaming.

"We need to go see my mom." The order rushed out of her mouth.

In the deepest parts of her soul, she knew that her mother would be able to tell her if what Michelle said was true. If she did allow Ryker to mark her the previous night, then that meant she was as good as mated. How would Ryker react after that? What would he want from her? They weren't necessarily close friends. Shit, she'd spent most of her life avoiding him.

Sara hastened up the mountain. Her mind raced around in circles through what Cici remembered of the dream. Dear God. He'd made her come until she'd passed out. And she- Oh no. Please God no. It had to be a dream because she had told him he was hers and ordered him to make her come.

"I think I'm gonna be sick." Cici groaned.

"Join the crowd." Came from Darius.

She glanced over her shoulder and caught him scrunching his face as if in pain. Poor guy. What the hell had she dragged him into?

When they got up to the cabins, she ran out of the car like a bat out of hell and tried to focus on staying calm. Yes. Calm. Or she'd blow a coronary at thirty.

Her mom sat at the kitchen table, writing notes. She glanced up and inhaled.

"Mom..." She struggled to get the words out past the knot in her throat. How could she have set her up that way? "Did Ryker come to my cabin last night? Do you know?"

"Yes. He stopped here first and then asked if you were in. I knew you were since you mentioned the wine I left for you so he headed your way." She smiled, eyes twinkling with joy.

She saw it then. The satisfied grin. Her mother set her up.

"But you knew I was drinking, mom. You knew I didn't want to be alone with him."

"Sweetheart, I didn't know you were concerned with drinking in front of Ryker."

"Mother! That's not what I mean. I was shit-faced and I," she gulped. "I thought I was dreaming."

"Was it a good dream?"

With her fingers gripping the chair across from her, she fought to stay calm, but her heart pounded so hard it was hard to listen to what she said. "Yes. It was great. Except it wasn't really a dream. And now people are telling me I'm marked but I don't recall being marked by him." She bit her lip. He'd kissed his way down her body, but not once had he bitten her, had he? "I don't understand where that's coming from."

Her mother blushed. "Darling, are you sure he didn't bite you? Anywhere?"

She frowned. God, was she really having this kind of conversation with her mother? "He may have nipped my inner thigh."

Her mother smiled softly. "That's usually where women are marked."

"Are you serious? Mo-ther!" She gasped. "How could he have done that while I was drunk?"

Her mom glanced down at the pad she'd been writing at, put the pen down softly next to it and sighed. "They're telling you the truth. I can scent he marked you."

How to process that? She tugged the chair she was trying to destroy with her grip and dropped onto the cushion.

"But why would he do that? He doesn't even want me."

Maybe it was a good thing their cabin was further up the mountain. Others wouldn't hear as she yelled at the top of her lungs. Her fear spiked in her chest. There was something going on that she was obviously unaware of or her brain had stopped working and she hadn't noticed.

Her mom's head lifted. She saw the excitement behind the wariness in her eyes. Her confusion grew but she reigned in her temper.

"Please," she begged with the last bit of patience she had, hands folded so tight in her lap her knuckles turned white. "Do you know why? Because right now, I'm damn confused. Ryker has never made it his business to come see me. Hell, he's never even called me to ask me on a date in forever."

She nodded. "You love him. Can't you just give it a chance?"

Um. No. "I need answers before I give anything my time. I refuse to give in just because he's decided to bite me. I'm not a shifter. The rules of his world don't apply to me."

There was only one thing to do. She stood to go.

She'd loved him since she was a kid. What started out as a crush had grown with each smile and each conversation into a deeper stronger love. However, that didn't mean they should mate. Her mother rushed behind her toward the door.

"I know you think you're not good enough for him, but you are."

That stopped Cici. She whirled around to face her. Fire bloomed on Cici's face. "It has nothing to do with being good enough. I know I'm good enough for someone out there, but Ryker needs one of his own kind to be his mate, mom. He's the Alpha. I am a human."

"You're beautiful, smart, and an amazing baker…"

"Mother! I don't have self-esteem issues. You don't need to tell me all the qualities that would make me a good wife for him. Did you hear me when I said he's the Alpha? The leader of this pack. Do you think it will be okay for him to have a hybrid child?"

"That doesn't happen in every case." Her mother argued.

"No. It doesn't. But the possibility exists. What if he has a child that turns out like Sara? With very little scent, can't shift and the only thing they have from the shifter side is the claws. What then?"

Eyes wide, her mother inhaled sharply. "I am sure he'd run the risk if he loves his mate. Not all our females are fertile. He'd run the risk of not fathering any cubs anyway. So why not be with the woman he loves?"

Did he love her? Her mind was too worked up over what she'd swore was the best dream of her life. It was now her worst nightmare. Fear and anger twisted knots in her heart. She refused to open doors to any kind of hope only to have them slammed in her face like when she'd been fifteen. She needed to see him. Without being drunk on four bottles of wine and half asleep.

"Give him a chance," she said.

Oh, she'd give him something all right. A punch in the gut or a kick in the balls was something. Stomping across the clearing, she pounded on his front door. Only a jerk would take advantage of a woman that was drunk. And in her own bed too!

Slam

"Ryker!"

Slam. Slam. Slam.

"Open up you miserable son of a bitch!"

Slam. Slam. Slam.

Nothing. She growled at the injustice of it all.

Slam. Slam. Slam.

Her anger diminished somewhat at the realization she wouldn't get a chance to yell at him at that point.

Restlessness settled in her. Her brain ordered her to move. It helped her think through big issues and being marked by the Alpha was definitely top of the food chain issue. She headed for a trail that led to the creek. As a kid everyone went swimming in there. But with the fall in full swing, the water was colder and most kids stopped their splashing in there, but she happened to like the cooler water. Her mind curled around a single thought: Marked by Ryker.

Ryker. He was the one she'd wanted since fifteen and the one man she couldn't have. She knew that. Yet her heart fluttered faster. Don't do it. She had to stop the small hope now, before she planned fairy tale ending and shit hit the fan. The big bad sexy growly Alpha was not for her.

Nearing the creek, she heard splashing. Her gaze swept over the water, but she saw nothing. The closer she got, the more she worried someone was in trouble. Once she stood by the end, she waited. A nervous breath later and a figure broke the surface. Their eyes met in an instant angry battle of wills.

"I was looking for you!"

Without thinking, she jumped into the waist deep water, making her way toward him. Ryker arched his brows in that annoying way that said she was being dramatic.

"Don't give me that look. You took advantage of me." She growled, hating the way the stupid water slowed her down.

He dove under.

"Ryker!" She yelled. "Get up here. I'm talking to you."

A pair of hands wrapped around her waist and tugged her down, further into the deep water. Instinctively, she grabbed on to his hair.

He rose again once the water hit shoulders. Their bodies stood flushed together, so tight you'd think they were born that way.

"I didn't take advantage of you." His voice, that deep churned gravel turned her hormones into a mess of longing.

"You did. I thought it was a dream." Christ. The things she'd said. The stuff she'd admitted to. Why did he do that to her?

"I didn't know you thought it was a dream. I thought you were finally being honest with both of us. We belong together." He answered as if reading her mind.

"You're an Alpha Shifter. I'm a human. Different species." She started to get annoyed again. He refused to apologize or even admit the error of his ways.

He caressed his hands under her wet shirt, sliding those strong fingers on her lower back. Biting back the moan in her throat, she stared deep into his ocean blue eyes.

"It doesn't matter. You were meant for me." His possessive tone and the lust sparking in his eyes left her breathless.

Her heartbeat doubled and she struggled to stay angry. "Ever heard of asking a woman on a date?"

"Would you? You've been running from me for years. You refuse to see me and you think I'd chance a date?" He argued back, holding her so close she could feel every single one of his muscles shifting down to the rock-hard erection poking her belly.

"I have not been running."

"You do know I can tell you're lying, right?"

Crap. "Whatever. I just refuse to be a notch on your tree post." She needed to fight his intense you-belong-to-me look and his firm but soft lips. Lips she remembered sucking her breast and licking her pussy so well she saw stars.

"Oh, Cici," he growled, exasperation showing clearly in his frown, "you are so much more than just a notch on my bed post. You're the only one for me."

Cici gulped. Focus. She needed to focus on what was important. He'd been wrong. "I was drunk out of my mind and you came into my house uninvited."

"You called for me. I sensed it."

"I thought I was dreaming."

"Your subconscious reached out to me."

Her breath caught at the back of her throat. He drew closer, moved his mouth just inches away.

Oh dear lord this wasn't going to end well. For the life of her, she couldn't find it in her to stop him. Her mind yelled for her to say 'no' but she didn't. Instead, she licked her lips. He groaned, closed the distance between their mouths, and finally kissed her.

It was wrong, but felt absolutely perfect. Though they were in a creek of cool water, the warmth from his body kept things hot. That and her body's fervent need spiking the temperature in her blood. Their kiss turned harder, rougher. Wild. Yes. It was exactly what she'd expect from Ryker. A possessive, dominating kiss that drove his tongue to rub over hers in a sensual mating dance meant to entice.

He tugged at her shirt, urging it off her. She should have stopped him then, but no. Need grew too strong. Passion flared too bright. And neither wanted to stop. He urged her backwards, towards a shallower side near the grass. The water dropped down to hip level and her back hit a rock wall. Waiting ended there. He licked down her neck, to her nipples and sucked one deep into his mouth. Explosions rocked her core with each suck. Tracing her way up to his wet hair, she moaned after the first bite on her nipple.

"Ryker..."

Her gaze was glued watching his tongue flick back and forth on her hard nipple. Then he did it on the other and she almost melted into the rock at her back. His mouth trailed down, lower and lower. He stopped at her quivering belly and ran circles over her belly button. After that he urged her pants down, panties and all.

"I need protection." He glanced over her shoulder. She guessed to the spot he'd left his pants.

"I'm on the pill." She took a breath of the cool afternoon air, filled her lungs to near bursting and rushed on.

"You're sure?" Her nipples scrunched up tighter from the sounds of the growly words.

Desire licked at her skin, raced to her pussy, and made her clit twitch. She nodded.

Their lips met in another blazing kiss that spread goose bumps all over her body. Once she widened her legs, he spread her pussy lips with his fingers and rubbed her clit.

She tore from his kiss and groaned. "Oh, God!"

He moved the hand further down, to drive his finger into her pussy. At that moment, she curled her fingers over his cock. The thick shaft stood hard long and wet from the water and his pre-cum.

She pumped him in her grasp. Ryker moaned. The sound further enhanced her need for him.

"Let me taste you," she said. "You've had a taste of me already."

Five

His eyes stared deep into hers, branding the deepest part of her soul. "Maybe later. I need inside you now."

"Please…"

"You're wet, sweetheart. So wet and ready." Those all-seeing eyes glowed with passion. "Do you want me?"

"Yes," she moaned, wiggling her hips on his fingers.

"Do you want me to fuck you and make you mine? No more excuses, Ciara. I want you. Tell me."

She breathed hard for a moment. Thinking about what he was asking her. Admitting that she wanted to be his didn't mean she had to stay. But she knew Ryker. He'd find a way to entice her to. He wouldn't ever force her. At that moment, her hormones ruled her mind and all she could think of was being his. Only his. Finally.

"Fuck me, Ryker. I need you."

She curled a leg around his waist, rubbed her pussy on his cock and hoped he'd get the idea. Thankfully, he did. He pressed her back into the wall. Gripped her ass with those large hands. At that same moment, she wound her other leg around his waist. And he drove deep. Balls deep. In a single mind-numbing drive, he stretched her pussy walls taut. The air pushed out of her lungs. A shocked gasp left her throat while her channel fluttered wildly around his driving shaft.

Desire pumped through her blood burning out her ability to think. All she could do was feel. Hands curled around his neck, she held on as he drove in and out of her. In. Out. Passion coiled in her tummy. His tongue sucked on her, pushed into her mouth and then propelled back. The same thing he was doing with his cock.

She fluttered her eyes open. Thick energy swirled around them. Its aggressive power seemed to have centered on Ryker. His moves turned wild. Rougher. Faster.

"Mine!" He growled.

She gulped at the dryness that took over her throat. Her pussy tightened around his cock. Water lapped at their sides, cold and clear. Loud moans broke through her lips. Heaven help her, but she would give up anything to be his.

"God, oh God!" She choked.

He licked at her neck, twirled his tongue in circles over her pounding pulse, and darkness took over the edges of her vision. The tension in her core twined into a ball, a pounding ball ready to break at any moment. Thrust after thrust he slammed into her, hitting the tension with each pound into her pussy. He sucked one of her nipples into his mouth. Bit down. Electricity burst from her nipple to her pussy. The ball cracked. Her world shattered so fast it turned into a blur.

She screamed or moaned. Or something. All she know is that once liquid bliss rushed her system like a direct hit of endorphins into her pleasure center. Her pussy squeezed tight at his cock. Shudders racked her spine. Breaths struggled into her lungs. Muscles felt liquefied and mini explosions continued to go off in her pussy. He pumped harder into her, using their slick bodies to increase speed. His cock thickened inside her, rubbing harder with each slam on her inner walls.

"Ryker..."

His facial lines tightened. For a second she thought he'd shift while still inside her, but he closed his eyes and she saw him struggle to keep his wolf at bay. His eyes snapped open and some of the tension receded from his face.

"You *will* be mine." He ground into her a final time and held himself tense. His body vibrated as he groaned his release. Warm semen filled her channel with his essence.

It took a long moment of intense breathing and him holding her against him for her to return to the real world. Uncurling from his gorgeous body, she tried to stand back on her own two feet. What a mess. He helped her stand, held her by her waist until her legs stopped trying to fold under her.

"I'm okay."

Ryker cupped her cheek. Tipped her head back and frowned. "Are you?"

Lie. Lie. Lie. "Yes."

Clothes. She had to put on some clothes and she might feel marginally less like an idiot. He stepped back, almost as if he'd known she needed some space. Trying not to think of what had just happened, for fear of freaking out completely, she made her way to the edge with her wet clothes in hand. She struggled into the sticky soaked fabric and muttered about being brain dead. It was her firm belief she was.

"Ciara, what are you doing?"

"Nothing." Fucking clothes! Why were they so hard to put on when wet? She kept her back to

Ryker. She couldn't fathom looking in the his eyes now that he'd messed her up one hundred percent for any other man. Before. She'd been emotional and had no idea what sex would be like with him. Now, though, she had gotten more than a taste and she was hooked.

Why did life have to be so unfair? She knew better than to get attached to him. For most of her life she'd been giving herself that pep talk to the point she could do it in her sleep.

"We need to talk, sweetheart." His voice sounded closer so she panicked.

She ran up to the side of the creek and turned around in a flash. Clumps of cold wet hair slapped the side of her face.

He was heading for the spot he'd left his clothes. She had to go. Now. "We don't need to talk. You need to…" His fully naked body filled her vision. Strong muscles, washboard abs, a bevy of tattoos lined his torso. Her brain screamed for her to go pet those muscles again. She screamed at her brain to stop torturing her. Stupid hormones were what got her into this to begin with. "You stay away from me. I'm not into games."

Before he said anything, she ran. Trees rushed by her sides. Her clothes clung to her like a second skin and the cool autumn air added a bite to raise the hairs on her arms. Forget her cabin, she ran for Sara's.

Confusion filled her mind and heart. She knew he'd catch up to her eventually, but right now she needed to think. How could things turn like this on her? Rushing into Sara's cabin, she bypassed both her and Darius at the living room and ran for her bathroom.

"What the hell?" Sara shouted. "Are you okay?"

"Ciara? What happened to you? You look like someone dumped you in a pool." Darius said from outside the bathroom door.

"I'm fine. If Ryker shows up, tell him I'm not ready to talk to him just yet." Cici ordered.

The last thing she needed was for him to say things she never imagined. Like mating. Relationships. Cubs. Christ, she needed a drink.

After a long and mentally draining shower, she put on the clothes Sara left for her on her bed. Her friends knew her so well. They'd left her alone to think. Now she needed them.

Both sat in the kitchen, quiet. They glanced up. Worried frowns marred both their brows.

"I'm fine." Cici sighed. Sara passed her a cup of coffee and Darius pushed a basket with pastries her way.

"So, what happened?" Darius patted her hand.

Cici sighed and sipped her coffee. "Apparently Ryker did mark me."

Sara's eyes went wide. "I knew it. But shit."

"Yeah." She snorted. "You can say that again."

Darius frowned. "What does this mean?"

"It means," Sara cut a pastry in half. "That she's engaged to the Alpha in the shifter world. Well, the Alpha of the Snow Mountain Pack. We're a pretty large pack in case you didn't know."

"Way to cheat on our fake engagement." Darius joked.

Laughter bubbled in her throat. This was why she needed her friends. They could always find a way to make her smile, even when she wanted to scream in frustration over her present situation.

"She never does things half-assed." Sara grinned.

"So what are you going to do?" Darius' dark gaze studied hers. "You know you love him. If it hadn't been for those girls and their jealous mamas telling you that he'd have to mate with a shifter, you'd probably have married him and had a dozen or more fur balls by now."

Babies. Lord that's the last thing she needed to think about when her biological clock had started to tick months back.

"He's right, Ciara. When you asked your mom to send you away to school so you wouldn't have to be here, I knew why you were doing it. I chose to go with you so you wouldn't be alone." She twirled the spoon in her coffee in circles. "We both know that even with all those miles and years between you, you still love the man. Heck, you dated a bunch of losers and even some nice guys trying to forget him, but that didn't work." She pinned her with her gaze, a sad smile on her face. "Remember?"

Of course she remembered. Not thinking of Ryker every day had almost killed her. But she fought to not visualize his eyes or his sexy mouth. To not relive their one and only date and every conversation they'd had. It was hard enough when she lived hundreds of miles away, but being this close was playing havoc with her heart. Him saying he wanted her, him marking her, those things gave a girl hope.

"He came by when you were in the shower. Said he'd give you some time to think, but that he'd be back later." Sara said.

Her mind turned into a mess. She returned to her cabin to continue the second half of her baking. If the shaking in her hands wasn't an indicator of how stressed out she was, the fact she almost forgot how to bake one of her signature cakes was another.

Thankfully, she'd remembered and shoved the cake in the oven, walking out of the kitchen to take a shower. She'd sat down to wait the last few minutes left on the second cake before it was due to come out of the oven when Michelle came by.

"Hi, I thought you might want to go for a walk." She smiled.

She liked Michelle for Chris. She was a sweetie and from what she knew had a bad relationship before him. She was happy they'd found each other. Though she didn't take to the change after they mated, Chris didn't care. Hell nobody cared. They were just happy her brother and his fiancée were happy.

"You going down by the creek?" There was no way in hell Ciara was going back that way.

"No, I thought maybe the flower pads."

Oh, she loved those. "You go and I'll meet you that way in a few. Cake number two is about to come out. Once I set it to cool I'll head in your direction."

"Okay, I may go a little by the hills, but no farther."

After Michelle left, she thought about Ryker. Maybe this was life trying to tell her she could finally have the man she wanted. He kept saying she was his. She'd have to figure out if he meant as his mate or just for sex.

Once the cake was out and cooling, Cici headed for the flower pads. She bypassed them when she didn't see Michelle. Then she heard a bloodcurdling scream that made her hair stand on end. Instinct took over. She ran toward the sound.

Trees opened up into a grassy hill where Michelle fought a man dragging her by the arm.

"Let me go you asshole!" Michelle kicked him in the shin, but he was big.

"I don't give a shit about restraining orders. You belong to me." He slapped her then.

Dark anger turned her vision red.

"I'm getting married. I was never yours. We dated for a few months, Todd. Let me go!" Michelle screamed.

Cici heard the panic in her voice.

"No!" He punched Michelle this time. She fell down unconscious.

"Hey!" Cici yelled running as fast as she could. "Let her go!"

"Mind your own business, bitch. She's mine and I'm taking her home." He slapped the unconscious Michelle. "Stupid bitch thinks she can run. I'll always find her."

Her blood boiled with rage. She was so close. Then she was in front of him as he readied to pick Michelle up. With a single hard kick, she sent him careening backwards, away from her body. She'd learned a lot from the shifters while growing up. One of those things had been how to defend herself.

Six

"You're going to regret that." He barked, jumping to his feet.

He came at her fast, but she dodged his fist and kicked his side. A meaty hand slapped his side rubbing the spot she'd kicked. He turned angry eyes her way.

"I'm gonna kill you and take her with me and you can't do anything to stop me." He hurtled himself at Cici. He moved a lot faster than she expected. He grabbed her wrist with one hand and dodged her leg with the other. Then he slapped her.

Pain radiated all over her cheek. She slammed a fist into his jaw. He howled in anger. Take that, asshole! Before she got a chance to grab her hand back, he took hold of her other wrist. Shoving her backwards, he pushed until her back hit a tree. His large body rubbed over hers. Disgusting.

"Maybe I'll have some fun with you before I take her home with me." He grinned, beady eyes staring at her breasts.

"You think you have the balls for that?" She watched his eyes widen. He probably didn't understand why she wasn't running scared. Adrenaline rushed through her veins, ignoring all signs of fear.

She knew what was coming. His head dropped closer. She reeled back and slammed forward, hitting their foreheads together. Cracking sounded. His loud yell made her wince. He ran back and away from her. Everything ran around in circles and her head pounded like a bitch.

"You crazy bitch!" He screamed repeatedly, rubbing his forehead while on his knees. Then he threw up. That was just nasty.

Ryker, Chris and a bunch of enforcers ran into the hill from the forest. That's when shit got real for Michelle's ex Todd. "You think I'm bad, you're about to meet your maker."

Chris shifted, dropping his large gray wolf on the intruder. The animal had no mercy. He bit and clawed at Todd without hesitation. Todd screamed, but the wolf didn't stop. He clawed at Todd's chest. Blood spurted everywhere. The wolf bit down repeatedly, tearing him limb from limb.

"Ahhhhh!"

Todd screamed multiple times until his life was torn from him by Chris' massive canines. Blood covered the grass in a dark red circle around his remains. Even then, the wolf wouldn't stop. She'd known her brother was strong. But seeing his animal in action was different. The air was pungent with fear, anger and blood. She was so taken by watching the wolf coat himself in the dead man's blood and continue to chew on his body as if he were a chew toy, that she almost missed Ryker reaching her side.

"Are you okay?" Ryker's deep gaze focused on her forehead. She rubbed it. Sure enough there was a bump the size of a golf ball on there. Lovely.

"I'm fine," she whispered, feeling all kinds of weird. They had to talk.

More people filled the hill clearing until the place was packed. Ryker twined his fingers with hers and pulled her forward. What the hell was he thinking? Had she been of a weaker constitution she may have fainted. Plus, her head pounded something fierce. Thank God for the shifter self-defense lessons she'd taken growing up and those she'd followed up while living in the city on her own. Kick-boxing rocked.

"Ryker, what do you want from me?" She asked once they were by the creek. The sun started to go down and the trees made it appear even darker outside.

He cupped her arms and turned her to face him. The look in his eyes left her breathless. "You. I only want you."

She bit her lip and thought about the girls and women that had told her all her life she wasn't right for him because she was the wrong species. "You need a shifter in your life."

He crowded her, pushing her back against the closest tree. Her back hit the unforgiving trunk and she whimpered in the back of her throat at the feel of his hard body pressing her front.

"I only need you, Cici. You're my everything."

She wanted to laugh at his silly words. Not feel her heart beat double time. "How can you say that? You hardly know me. We went on one date, Ryker. One. And we were teens."

He lifted a hand and ran his fingers into her hair, cupping her neck and caressing her jaw with his thumb. "I know you are it for me, Cici. I knew it the first time I saw you. My animal and my instinct to connect with my mate told me it was you."

She swallowed back the knot forming in her throat. Most of her life she'd dreamed of hearing him say that. She wanted to be his everything. But she'd been jaded with the years of being told humans were not good enough for a shifter. "I thought humans were too weak to be shifter mates?"

He shook his head, lowering his face to brush his lips over hers. The world felt amazingly right at that moment. Like no matter what happened, it would all be okay for her.

"No. I know we have some people who think humans aren't good enough, but we don't all think that way." He swept his tongue over her lips in a seductive caress that made her panties soaked. "You're one of the strongest women in the world, Cici. Human or not, I want you." His gaze pierced her. "It's time to choose. Are you giving me permission to bite you and take you for myself, or will you ignore how we both feel and move on?"

Fuck. Fuck. Fuck. Trying to remember her name was hard enough without adding difficult thinking like this.

Her mind reeled against leaving Ryker now that she realized how he felt. She had to take a chance. This might be the time for them. She pushed the insecurity over what others thought and focused on him. Ryker. The man she had loved since she was a kid.

"Come on, Cici," he said, rubbing his erection on her. Passion nearly blindsided her.

Her mind screamed 'live for today and forget everything else.'

"Yes..." she groaned, curling her arms around his neck and tugging his head closer. "I...Okay. Let's take a chance on this. On us."

His lips lifted in a feral smile that made her breath hitch in her chest. "That's my girl."

She licked her lips and leaned forward. "So bite me already."

"My pleasure, baby." He took her lips in a hard, demanding claiming. There was little time for thinking. Feeling took control. She rubbed her tongue over his, mimicking the acting of lovemaking. Explosions rocked her insides until she felt like she was melting down to the bone.

She gripped his hair in her fists, holding on to him for dear life. The sounds of ripping and tearing were music to her ears. Soon, cool air caressed her naked body from head to toe.

He pulled back, away from her and swept his heated gaze down her curves.

"You are so fucking sexy."

She watched him jerk out of his clothes in the blink of an eye. "I think you win the sexier of the two by way more votes," she breathed.

He shook his head and lifted her into his arms. "No way, beautiful," he said, kissing her neck and strolling to the creek. He walked into shoulder deep water by a rock where she loved to sit and wet her legs. Then he put her back on her feet. "Your body is soft, curvy, and sexy. There's no competition."

She squeaked as he lifted her up to the rock seat that put her crotch level with his head. "You're crazy!"

"Crazy? No way, love. Imaginative." He curled his arms around her large thighs and held her in place. "Look how wet and pink you are," he growled. "So fucking perfect."

Vibrations rocked her insides with pleasure over his words. One glance at his face and moisture slid from her slit. He looked ready to devour her.

"Ryker," her voice hitched, her breaths puffing out in short bursts. "I need you to do something soon or I'll hurt you."

He chuckled and lowered his head between her legs. The first lick and tension unraveled slowly at the pit of her belly. She gasped. "Oh, my..."

There was no thoughts as the cool water lapped at her butt or the normally cooler air hit her heated flesh. Instead, she focused on his hot tongue gliding up and down her folds. The amazing feel of his lips suckling on her engorged clit.

A loud groan rolled up her throat. She grasped his hair with her wet hands, holding the strands in a deathly grip.

He slid a finger into her, fucking her so damn slowly with the digit she wanted to scream. Her leg muscles tightened. Her belly quivered and her nipples pebbled into tiny points.

He lavished her folds with multiple licks and sucks. Air pounded hard in her chest, fighting its way into her lungs. She swore he rubbed his entire face on her pussy. It was insanely erotic to feel the bristles of his beard on her pussy. No man had ever done that to her. Then there were the growls. Every time he licked, he growled. The vibrations electrified her blood to boiling level. She choked out a gasp as her body tensed, so close to the edge she couldn't think even if her life depended on it. Then he sucked on her clit hard.

"Ryker!" She screamed. The tension in her belly exploded into a crescendo of light and pleasure.

Blasts of wondrous pleasure cascaded outward to her limbs until she swore she'd lost all ability to move. Stars lined her vision. She blinked repeatedly trying to bring herself back to reality.

Ryker pounced out of the pool and landed above her. She hadn't seen him do that before. Water dripped down his muscular body, down his powerful abs and thick shaft. Holy fuck. That was amazing. That was unreal. That was…Hot as hell!

She whimpered. His golden gaze melted her to the rock. Fur sprouted from his sideburns. She opened her mouth to say something but was left breathless when he picked her up and repositioned her to be on all four.

He caressed his claws down her back. He'd lost some of his tenuous control on his animal.

"I need inside you."

Yeah. Even his voice was a low growl. He licked the back of her shoulder, nipping as he slipped the head of his cock into her.

"Oh, Ryker," she groaned. He felt so big. Hot. Throbbing.

Her pulse pounded in her ears. She clawed at the grass under her hands, looking for leverage. He continued driving his cock into her, stretching her vaginal walls taut.

Once he was fully seated, he bit her earlobe, pulled back and quickly drove forth. He gripped her hips hard, the tips of his claws digging into her flesh.

Another plunge and she saw stars. He propelled back and pushed in, balls deep.

"Fuck, baby. I love being inside you." He growled. "I love the tight feel of your pussy." Another pull and drive forth. "I want to fill you with my seed, Ciara." His breath brushed the back of her neck. Another plunge and she gasped out a groan. "I want my scent in you. On you. I want my seed to take root in your belly. You're the only one I want."

She blinked. The things he said hadn't been said to her during sex. "You…what?"

He growled and thrust harder, faster. "I want to fuck your sweet cunt until I come deep inside you. Until I get you pregnant with my baby. I want you mine and nobody else's."

She curved her back, plastering to his front. "Please…Ryker…"

"Tell me you want that. Tell me you want me to fuck you raw. To come inside your tight little pussy and fill you with my seed. Tell me you want to have my babies."

"God, yes!"

She couldn't have expected that those two words would unleash the animal in him. His thrust lost all control. He increased the pace to an unreal speed. Her lungs burned trying to get air in them.

She inhaled sharply before her world broke. Pleasure swept through her in a wave of electric release. She screamed, her body gripping and clenching around his cock.

He growled by her ear. His thrusts slowing down. "Mine!"

His teeth were on her shoulder, biting down. The sharp sting of the bite only added to the wave of pleasure rolling through her. His canines embedded in the back of her shoulder as she continued to ride her release. Blood rushed to her head. He growled again. A loud howl with his teeth still in her shoulder, signaling his reach of release. It was so powerful that it sent a new set of vibrations down her body as he came. His cock throbbed inside her, his heated cum coating her insides.

She leaned her head back, into his head as he licked the bite on her shoulder. "You're mine now, sweetheart."

For so long, she'd refused to believe Ryker could ever be hers. She refused to believe they could have a future. All because of hateful people that didn't want her to be his mate. Now she had the chance to have the future she'd always wanted. Yes, there were numerous questions in her head, but she couldn't reject him. Ryker wanted her. She wanted him. This wasn't a question of her feeling insecure because of her body. She had curves and she loved every one of them. This was a question of her species. Screw what others thought. Happiness was being handed to her on a silver platter.

She smiled. "I think I can live with that."

* * *

The next morning, Ciara was about to ready for another day of baking when Ryker shook his head and grabbed her by the hand.

"No way, sweetheart. You're coming with me," he said, tugging her out the door. He took her to the flower patch to talk.

"What's going on?" She was still getting used to the fact he'd bitten her the night before. Multiple times. Talk about an aggressive male. He'd even growled and howled when he came. The memory sent shudders racing down her spine.

He lifted her hand to his lips and winked. "You'll see."

Soon, a large crowd of his enforcers started showing up from between the trees. She frowned, unsure what was going on. Nerves kept her immobile. More and more people gathered around them. Shit, what the hell was going on?

A glance at Ryker and all she got was a smile. Figured. The jerk wasn't going to give her any clues on what was happening. When she swore everyone in the pack was in the area, Ryker cleared his throat. All eyes trained on them.

"Ciara is mine. My mate. Our pack's future. Anyone who has a problem with this can challenge me now."

Deadly silence filled the area. Acid from the bile that hit the back of her throat rushed up her windpipe. One by one, the enforcers walked up to her, got on their knees, and lowered their necks in submission. She glanced at Ryker, unsure what to do. Each of the enforcers said the same thing to her.

"Accept our loyalty as our Alpha's mate."

Tears clogged the back of her throat. More people got on their knees and displayed their neck. She had a hard time holding it together. The pack had accepted her. The crazy thing was that she'd been questioning her decision about them from the moment she'd opened her eyes that morning. Had she made the right move?

Standing there with a dry throat and no words to come close to how surreal everything felt, she made her decision. If he wanted her, she was his. No more, no less.

Chris had carried Michelle to be seen by the local doctor the previous day, so he was missing. Once everyone had pledged their loyalty, he took her by the hand again and led her down another path. They walked hand in hand in complete silence to what had been her favorite spot as a kid. It was a huge old wild fig tree with a massive trunk and so many branches she loved to stare at it for hours.

They sat down by the trunk and for a moment neither said anything. She rubbed her sweaty palms down the sides of her pants.

Ryker grabbed her hand in his and met her gaze. "I love you, Ciara."

The words pierced her heart and filled her with warmth. "You do?"

He nodded. "Have since forever it seems."

She cleared her throat. Nerves got the best of her. "Be real."

"Seeing the prettiest girl smile just for me, made my heart race only for you from then on."

Wow. Her feelings for him broke out of the box she'd locked them up. "I…"

"I know you love me. You don't need to say it." His blue eyes focused on her lips. "But I need you to give us a chance. I know you said you would last night, but now, with your hormones no longer making your decisions for you, I am asking again. I want you to be with me. I don't want anyone else."

God. How could she ever have doubted him? Still, inklings of questions dirtied her happiness. "Ryker. I do, love you. But how do we know this is right for us? We lead two different lives."

He reached into his pocket and pulled out an old napkin. She frowned. Watched him unfold the paper with so much care you'd think it was made of gold. Then he handed it to her. Her heart stopped. Her fingers shook. And she knew then he really did love her.

"It's the napkin from our picnic." She mumbled.

Their one date. She'd arrived early to set up the picnic. In her restless wait, she had doodled his name with little hearts a ton of times on one of the cloth napkins her mom had packed for them. She had shoved it into the picnic basket when they'd left, so she didn't know how he got his hands on it.

"Mom!" She gasped.

He lifted a hand. Slowly, he caressed her cheek with his fingers. "She gave it to me after you went away for school. Told me you'd come back because you loved me."

It was then she stopped kidding herself. She opened her mouth and let her feelings loose. "I do love you. I have for too many years to count."

"I'm sorry if my telling you that night that my mate had to be here with me scared or upset you. I only wanted you to know what was coming."

She shook her head. Sad that she'd let other people's words ruin their once budding relationship. "It wasn't you. Before you showed up the day of our picnic, some girls had told me you couldn't be serious because I wasn't a shifter. I guess it always stayed with me. They said you needed a shifter for a mate and I…I refused to believe that a human was good enough for an Alpha."

He shook his head. "Good enough? You're more than that. You're perfect. Everything about you is perfection, Ciara. From your gorgeous eyes to your voluptuous curves. I love it. All of it."

"You mean that, don't you?" She asked in awe.

"I do. And while I want to ask you to stay, I won't. I want you to choose the path yourself, but know my heart belongs to you. And if you don't stay, there will never be another woman for me. If you do stay, I won't push you to lead with me, but let's be together." He said softly. "Please."

Happiness bounced around in her chest. "What if I want to be your mate in every sense of the word and lead the pack with you?"

She found herself on her back with a smiling Ryker staring down at her. "Then I can make that happen. Anything you want, sweetheart."

"I'll stay with you, Ryker. I love you."

His head dropped. He nuzzled her lips with his. "I love you too. I'm glad I finally get to keep my mate."

She was beyond happy that the man she'd wanted and loved for so long loved her back just as hard.

Epilogue

"Don't they look amazing?" She smiled.

"Gorgeous."

"Fantastic."

Sara and Darius sighed at the same time. Chris and Michelle twirled at the center of the dance floor, eyes glued to each other. They exuded happiness and love. It was a lovely thing to see.

Her mind played back the events from the past evening. Though they tried not to over do it, she saw the happiness in her mom and step dad now that she'd agreed to stay. Chris and Michelle were over the moon. And for the first time in her life, she had the man she wanted to be with forever.

Darius suddenly perked up in his seat. One of the new enforcers headed toward them. Tall, golden skinned and muscled to boot, he grinned at Darius.

"Have you had a chance to see the flower pads?"

"No, but I'd love to." He grinned.

Sara stared at a particular new enforcer on the other side of the room. He was busy talking to another girl, but every few moments he'd glance up and he would meet her gaze.

"Go talk to him."

"Yeah. Like I have a death wish or something," she muttered. "I'm going to go get another drink. I think I'm probably the only one not getting laid tonight."

Cici laughed, watching her head for the outside bar.

"Care to dance?" Ryker whispered in her ear. Her body went into instant overdrive.

"With you? Always."

A slow song played as she curled her arms around his neck. He hugged her tight, running his hands up and down her lower back. Their gazes met and lava heated her aroused core. His lips meet hers in a soft brush. She wanted more.

"Know what I feel like doing?"

His lips tipped up in a sexy grin. "What, my love?"

"Going for a swim."

His eyes brightened with arousal. Another kiss followed her words. This one opening the doors to the pleasure she knew she'd have soon. Heart near bursting with happiness, she held on to the only man she'd ever loved.

The End

About the Author

New York Times and USA Today Bestselling Author Milly Taiden (AKA April Angel) loves to write sexy stories. How sexy? So sexy they will surely make your ereader sizzle. Usually paranormal or contemporary, her stories are a great quick way to satisfy your craving for fun heroines with curves and sexy alphas with fur.

Milly lives in New York City with her hubby, their boy child and their little dog "Needy Speedy". She's aware she's bossy, is addicted to shoe shopping, chocolate (but who isn't, right?) and Dunkin' Donuts coffee.

She loves to meet new readers!

Sign up for Milly's newsletter for latest news!

http://eepurl.com/pt9q1

Find out more about Milly Taiden here:

Email: millytaiden@gmail.com
Website: http://www.millytaiden.com
Facebook: http://www.facebook.com/millytaidenpage
Twitter: https://www.twitter.com/millytaiden

If you liked this story, you might also enjoy by Milly Taiden:

Sassy Mates Series

Scent of a Mate *Sassy Mates Book One*
A Mate's Bite *Sassy Mates Book Two*
Unexpectedly Mated *Sassy Mates Book Three*
The Mate Challenge *Sassy Mates Book Four – Coming Soon*

Federal Paranormal Unit

Wolf Protector *Federal Paranormal Unit Book One*
Dangerous Protector *Federal Paranormal Unit Book Two*

Black Meadow Pack

Sharp Change *Black Meadows Pack Book One*
Caged Heat *Black Meadows Pack Book Two*

Paranormal Dating Agency

Twice the Growl *Book One*
Geek Bearing Gifts *Book Two*
The Purrfect Match *Book Three*
Curves 'Em Right *Book Four*
Tall Dark and Panther *Book Five – Coming Soon*

Night and Day Ink - Shorts

Bitten by Night
Seduced by Days
Mated by Night
Taken by Night

Other Works

Wolf Fever
Fate's Wish
Wynter's Captive
Sinfully Naughty Vol. 1
Club Duo (Laila, Elissa, Laura, Cristina)
Don't Drink and Hex
Hex Gone Wild
Hex and Kisses
Bratty Lioness Tamer
Alpha Owned

If you enjoyed the book, please consider leaving a review, even if it's only a line or two; it would make all the difference and would be very much appreciated.

Thank you!

9840954R00055

Printed in Great Britain
by Amazon.co.uk, Ltd.,
Marston Gate.